THIS LITTLE TIGER BOOK BELONGS TO:

_____

_____

_____

For Eleanor Troth &
Emily Peopall
~ *J.S.*

For Jane,
who *loves* Christmas!
~ *T.W.*

LITTLE TIGER PRESS
An imprint of Magi Publications
1 The Coda Centre, 189 Munster Road,
London SW6 6AW
First published in Great Britain 1998
This paperback edition published 2007
Text copyright © Julie Sykes 1998
Illustrations copyright © Tim Warnes 1998
Julie Sykes and Tim Warnes have asserted their rights
to be identified as the author and illustrator of this work
under the Copyright, Designs and Patents Act, 1988.
Printed in China
ISBN 978-1-84506-672-7

2 4 6 8 10 9 7 5 3 1

LITTLE TIGER PRESS
London

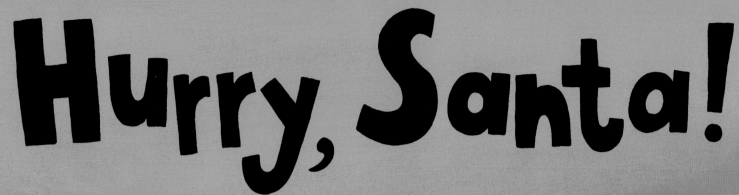

Hurry, Santa!

by Julie Sykes

illustrated by Tim Warnes

It was Christmas Eve, and Santa's busiest
time of year.

"ZZZzzz," he snored from under his quilt.

"Wake up!" squeaked Santa's little mouse,
tugging at his beard. "Hurry, Santa! You
shouldn't be late tonight."

"Ouch!" cried Santa, sitting up and rubbing
his chin. "Goodness, is that the time?
My alarm clock didn't go off, and
I've overslept."

Santa leapt out of bed and began to pull
on his clothes. He was in such a hurry that
he put both feet down one pants leg and
fell flat on his face.

"Hurry, Santa!" meowed his cat. "You shouldn't be late tonight."

"No, I shouldn't," agreed Santa, struggling up. "I shouldn't be late delivering the presents."

When he was dressed, Santa hurried outside to
his sleigh. He picked up the harness and tried to
put it on the reindeer.
But the reindeer weren't there!
"Oh no!" cried Santa. "Where have they gone?"

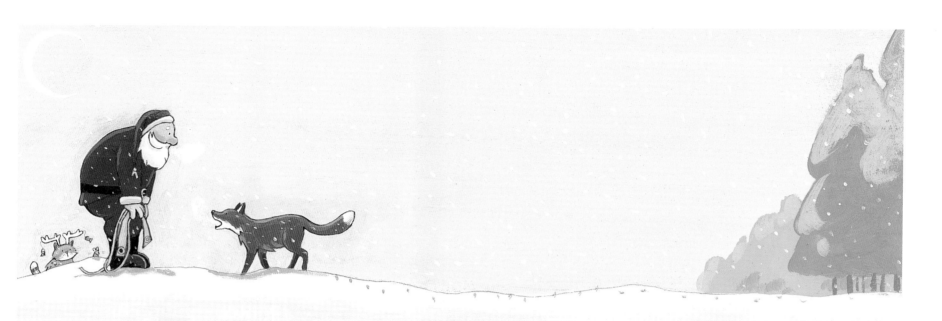

"The reindeer are loose in the woods. You'd better catch
them before they wander away," called Fox. "Hurry, Santa,
you shouldn't be late tonight."
"No, I shouldn't," agreed Santa, running toward the trees.

Deep in the woods, the reindeer
were having a snowball fight.
"Aaaaah!" cried Santa loudly,
as a snowball hit him in the face.

"Hurry, Santa," hooted Owl. "You don't have time to play in the snow. You shouldn't be late tonight."

"I wasn't playing!" said Santa, indignantly. "Come on, you silly reindeer, we've got work to do."

At last Santa was ready to leave. With a crack
of his whip and a jingle of bells he steered the
sleigh toward the moon.
"Go, Reindeer, go!" he shouted. "We can't
be late tonight."

Around the world they flew, delivering presents
to every child.

"Down again," called Santa, turning the sleigh
toward a farm.

"Hurry, Santa!" answered the reindeer. "We're
miles from anywhere, and the night's nearly over."

"I'm doing my best," said Santa, flicking the reins.

Before Santa could stop them, the reindeer
went faster.
"Whoa," Santa cried, but it was too late.
Landing with a bump, the sleigh skidded
crazily across the snow.
"Ooooh deeeaaar!" cried Santa in alarm.

CRASH!
The sleigh stopped in a ditch.
Santa scrambled to his feet and rubbed
his bruised bottom. "Nothing broken,"
he boomed. "But we must hurry!"

When the reindeer had untangled themselves,
everyone tried to dig out the sleigh. They tugged
and they pulled, and they pushed as hard as they
could, but the sleigh was completely stuck.

"It's no good," wailed the reindeer. "We can't move this sleigh on our own."

"We must keep trying," said Santa. "The sky is getting lighter, and we're running out of time."

Just then a loud neigh made Santa jump in surprise.
Trotting toward him was a very large horse.
"Hurry, Santa!" she neighed. "You still have presents
to deliver. *I'll* help you move your sleigh."
Everyone pulled together, even Santa's little mouse,
but it was no good. The sleigh was still stuck.

"Hurry, Santa!" called the rooster from the gate.
"You must be quick. It's nearly morning."
"I am *trying* to hurry," puffed Santa. "I have to
deliver the last of the presents on time."
Then suddenly the sleigh began to move . . .

. . . and Santa shot backward,
cheering loudly.
"Hurry, Santa!" called all the animals.
"The sun's rising. You have to be on your
way before the children wake up."

"Yes," agreed Santa. "It's nearly Christmas Day!"

It was a close call, but by dawn Santa
had managed to deliver every present.
"We did it!" yawned Santa. "I wasn't . . ."

Santa stopped talking and stared at his sack in dismay. At the very bottom there was still one present left. "Oh no, how awful!" he cried. "I've forgotten someone!"

Then Santa noticed that the animals were
laughing.
"That present is for *you*. It's from all of us,"
said the reindeer.

"Hurry, Santa!" added Santa's little mouse.
"Open your present. It's Christmas Day!"
"Yes, I will," chuckled Santa. "Now, I wonder
what it is . . ."